Published by Ladybird Books Ltd.
A Penguin Company
Penguin Books Ltd., 80 Strand London WC2R 0RL
Penguin Books Australia Ltd., Camberwell, Victoria, Australia
Penguin Books (NZ) Ltd., Private Bag 102902, NSMC, Auckland, New Zealand
2 4 6 8 10 9 7 5 3 1
LADYBIRD and the device of a ladybird are trademarks of Ladybird Books Ltd.
Printed in Italy
www.ladybird.co.uk

DISNEY'S
BROTHER
BEAR

Ladybird

Long ago, when ice and snow covered the earth, a boy named Kenai went on a magical journey and learned about brotherly love and the love that connects all things.

Kenai and the people of his village believed that the spirits of their ancestors lived in the lights of the Northern sky. It was these spirits that guided the villagers throughout their lives.

Tanana, the village wise woman, spoke to the spirits to learn what quality each person should use to make their decisions in life. Kenai's was love, and its symbol was a bear. Tanana gave Kenai a special necklace called a totem. Kenai's totem had the image of a bear on it.

But Kenai hated bears – they frightened people and stole food from the village. When Kenai's brother, Sitka, died in an accident while hunting a bear, Kenai's hatred grew stronger. He wanted to find the bear and take revenge.

Kenai's other brother, Denahi, tried to stop him, reminding him of his totem and its meaning.

"Don't upset the spirits," Denahi warned.

But Kenai tore the totem from his neck and stormed off.

"I've got to stop him," said Denahi, going after his brother.

The brothers didn't know it, but Sitka was watching over Kenai. Sitka saw his brother find the bear and kill it.

Suddenly lights flashed, and animal spirits swirled from the sky. Kenai saw Sitka as a spirit eagle, then felt himself being lifted into the lights.

A moment later, he was back on the ground. But he didn't know that Sitka had changed him into a bear.

Meanwhile, Denahi was still looking for Kenai. When he saw a bear standing beside Kenai's torn clothes, he feared his youngest brother had also been killed by a bear.

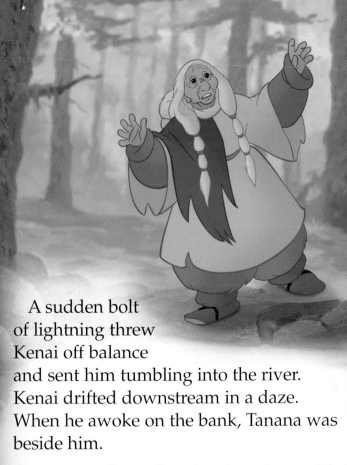

A sudden bolt
of lightning threw
Kenai off balance
and sent him tumbling into the river.
Kenai drifted downstream in a daze.
When he awoke on the bank, Tanana was
beside him.

Kenai tried to talk to her, but she couldn't
understand his growls. And Kenai couldn't
understand why his body felt so strange.
Tanana gently explained that Sitka's spirit
had changed him into a bear.

When Tanana saw how upset this made Kenai, she told him that he could change back only if he found Sitka. "Go to the mountain where the lights touch the earth," she said. Then she was gone.

Wandering around, Kenai saw two moose named Rutt and Tuke arguing with each other. Kenai tried to explain that he was a man, not a bear, but they just laughed at him.

Frustrated, Kenai left, and soon he met a lively bear cub named Koda who decided to help Kenai. As the little bear chattered on, a hunter appeared – it was Denahi! Koda fled into an ice cave.

Of course, Denahi didn't recognise Kenai. All he saw was the bear he thought had killed his brother. He attacked Kenai, who escaped to the cave where Koda was hiding.

When Denahi was gone, Koda told Kenai about something called "the Salmon Run." He had become separated from his mother, and wanted Kenai to take him there.

"There are tons of fish, and every night we watch the lights touch the mountain," he told Kenai excitedly.

Suddenly Kenai remembered Tanana's words. That was where he had to go!

When they started out the next morning, Kenai was annoyed by Koda's constant chattering. Kenai really didn't want to be travelling with the cub but he had no other option. He would just have to put up with Koda.

Along the way they met Rutt and Tuke, who told them that the hunter was still tracking them.

Suddenly Kenai had an idea to
throw Denahi the hunter off their trail.
Moments later, he and Koda were
riding mammoths. Mammoth
footprints would hide their tracks!

Next morning, Kenai and Koda
discovered they were lost. Kenai
blamed Koda, who was so upset that
he started to run off.

Kenai followed Koda to an abandoned cave with handprints on the wall – human handprints. Sadly, he put his hairy paw over one. Then his eyes moved to a painting of a hunter and a bear.

"Those monsters are really scary," said Koda, beside him. His heart sinking, Kenai realised that Koda was talking about the hunter, not the bear.

Kenai and Koda continued through the forest, and Kenai's mood lifted when Koda said they were close to the Salmon Run. But first they had to get through a place that seemed like a valley of fire.

"Kenai! Look out!" Koda suddenly screamed. Denahi had found them!

Kenai slammed his front paws to the ground, releasing a blast of steam that sent Denahi reeling. Then Kenai grabbed Koda in his mouth. Zigzagging through the spitting steam, they managed to lose Denahi and make their way across a log bridge leading out of the valley.

"Why do they hate us?" Koda asked Kenai, as they trundled through the forest once more.

"We're bears," Kenai replied. "You know… killers."

"But he attacked us!" Koda protested.

Kenai knew Koda was right. But he knew how the hunter felt, too. How could he explain that?

Suddenly gulls flew overhead, crying "Fish! Fish! Fish!" They were at the Salmon Run!

As huge bears crowded around the newcomers, Kenai felt frightened. But the bears were friendly and they welcomed him like part of the family. Kenai soon felt surrounded by warmth and love. It was the brotherly love from this extended family of bears.

Later, the bears gathered to talk about how they had spent the year. Koda described how he and his mother had been frightened by a hunter and got separated. Koda told everyone that he was sure she was OK, though.

Kenai listened in horror to the story. Then, he slowly began to realise that the hunter Koda was describing was himself as a human. Kenai immediately knew that Koda's mother was not alright at all. She was the bear he had killed.

Kenai tried to explain to Koda, to tell him that he had once been a man and that he now realised that he had done something very wrong.

"Your mother's not coming," Kenai said, sadly.

"No," Koda sobbed, running away from Kenai. "No!"

After realising Koda would be better off
on his own. Kenai headed out alone until
he found the mountain where the lights
touched the earth, where he begged the
spirits for help. Suddenly a huge shadow
loomed in the moonlight. It was Denahi!
He was filled with rage as he thundered
towards Kenai. Denahi lunged at Kenai
and brought him to the ground.

All at once Koda rushed at them,
knocking Denahi off balance. "Leave him
alone!" yelled Koda.

Leaping up, Denahi raced after the cub.

All Denahi heard was a roar. He grabbed his spear and turned – and gasped at what he saw.

A giant eagle had the bear in its talons. As the bird set him down, swirling lights surrounded Kenai and he became human again. At the same time, the eagle spirit changed into Sitka.

Kenai, in human form, reached out to Koda. "It's me," he said gently. As his little bear brother leapt into his arms, Kenai turned to his human brothers. "He needs me," he said simply. Kenai had decided to live his life as a bear.

"It's all right," said Denahi. "You'll always be my brother."

As Kenai became a bear again, the spirit of Koda's mother appeared and shared a hug with her cub. Koda knew that everything was going to be alright.

Kenai understood the meaning of his totem at last. He knew that now he would always let love guide his actions. One day his paw print would join the handprints of his human ancestors on a cave wall, showing that love connected them all, human and animal, forever.